# POTATOES AND ME

Words by John Coy • Pictures by Carolyn Fisher

Alfred A. Knopf • New York

For my dad, who taught me how to grow potatoes, and everything else.
-J.C.

Thanks to Norton Stillman for the idea.

For Stevie. -C.F.

THIS IS A BORZOI BOOK PUBLISHED BY ALFRED A. KNOPF

Published in the United States by Alfred A. Knopf,
an imprint of Random House Children's Books,
a division of Random House, Inc., New York,
and simultaneously in Canada by Random House of Canada Limited, Toronto.
Distributed by Random House, Inc., New York.
www.randomhouse.com/kids
KNOPF, BORZOI BOOKS, and the colophon
are registered trademarks of Random House, Inc.
Library of Congress Cataloging-in-Publication Data
Coy, John, 1958-
Two old potatoes and me / words by John Coy; pictures by Carolyn Fisher.
p. cm.
Summary: After a young girl finds two old potatoes at her father's house, they plant and tend them to see if they will have new potatoes in September.
ISBN 0-375-82180-5 (trade) - ISBN 0-375-92180-X (lib. bdg.)
[1. Fathers and daughters-Fiction. 2. Potatoes-Fiction. 3. Divorce-Fiction.] I. Fisher, Carolyn, ill. II. Title.
PZ7.C839455Tw 2003
[E]-dc21
2002043261
Printed in the United States of America
June 2003
10 9 8 7 6 5 4 3 2 1
First Edition

Last spring at my dad's house, I found
two old potatoes
in the back of the cupboard. 
They were so OLD,
sprouts were growing
from their eyes.

"Gross."
I tossed them in the TRASH.

"Wait,"

DAD said.

"I think we can grow new potatoes with those."

"I'll call your Grandpa.

He'll know."

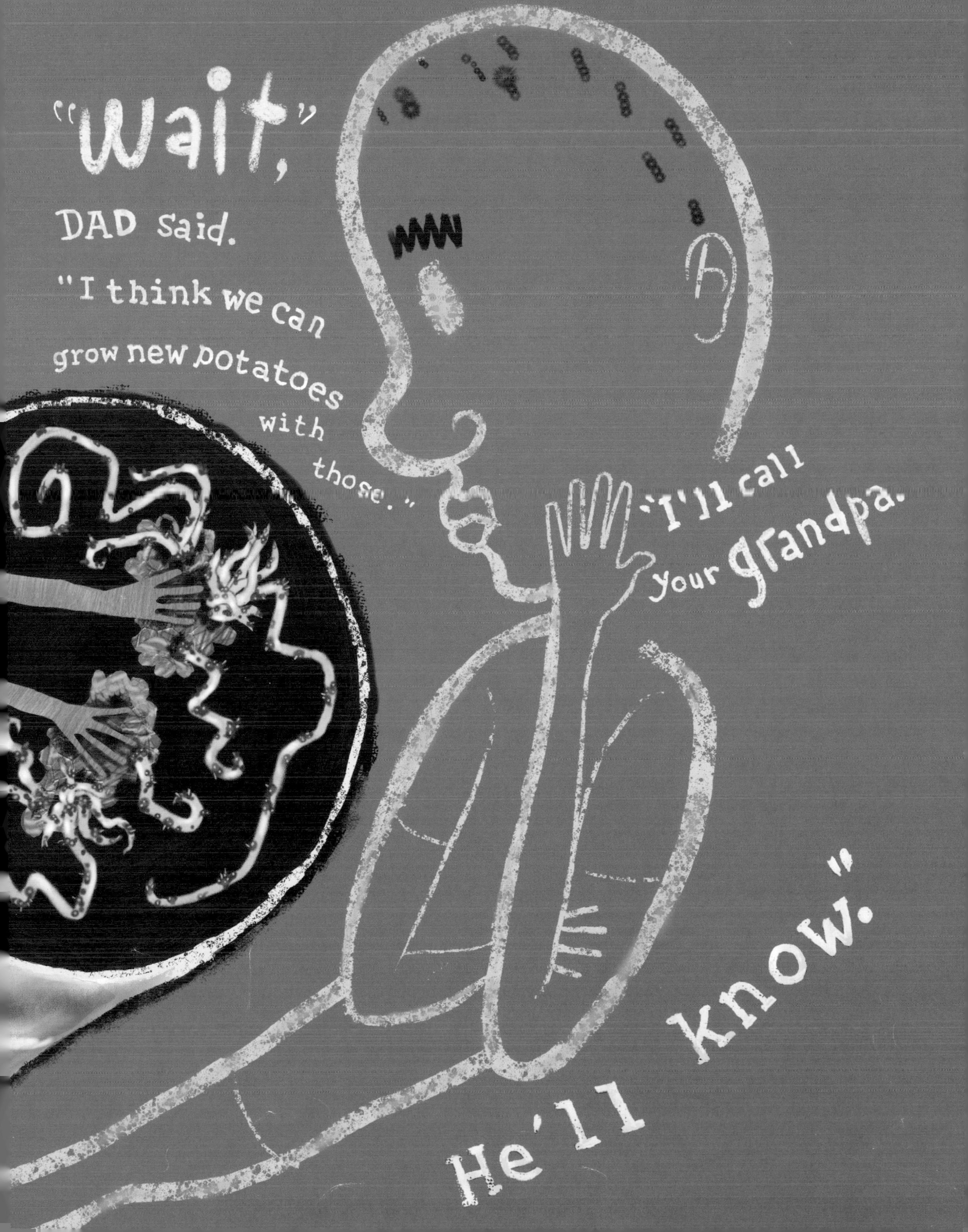

After talking with Grandpa, Dad and I took the potatoes

We dug.

to the sunniest spot in the garden.

We picked out rocks.

We raked the soil smooth.

Dad carefully cut the potatoes into nine pieces with his jackknife.

I made sure each piece had at least one yellow sprout.

Dad dug nine small holes. I put a piece of potato, with the eye facing up, in each hole.

Then I covered them with dirt to make little hills.

Dad got the hose

and I watered gently.

In May,
green plants poked up
like caterpillars unfolding.
We got down
on our knees
and picked weeds.
We shoveled compost onto each hill.

"Won't that smother the plants?"

"No. They'll grow through it."

"Are we really going to get new potatoes from old potatoes?"

"I think so," said Dad.

IN JUNE,

the plants grew bigger,

violet flowers blossomed,

and we added more compost.

When we watered,
I accidentally sprayed my dad with the hose.

He laughed

and

sprayed me back.

IN JULY, when the plants were as tall as my waist, we picked potato beetles off the leaves.

I dropped them into a pail of soapy water.

"Gross

"We have to do this," Dad said.

"Otherwise, the bugs will eat the leaves and the potatoes won't grow."

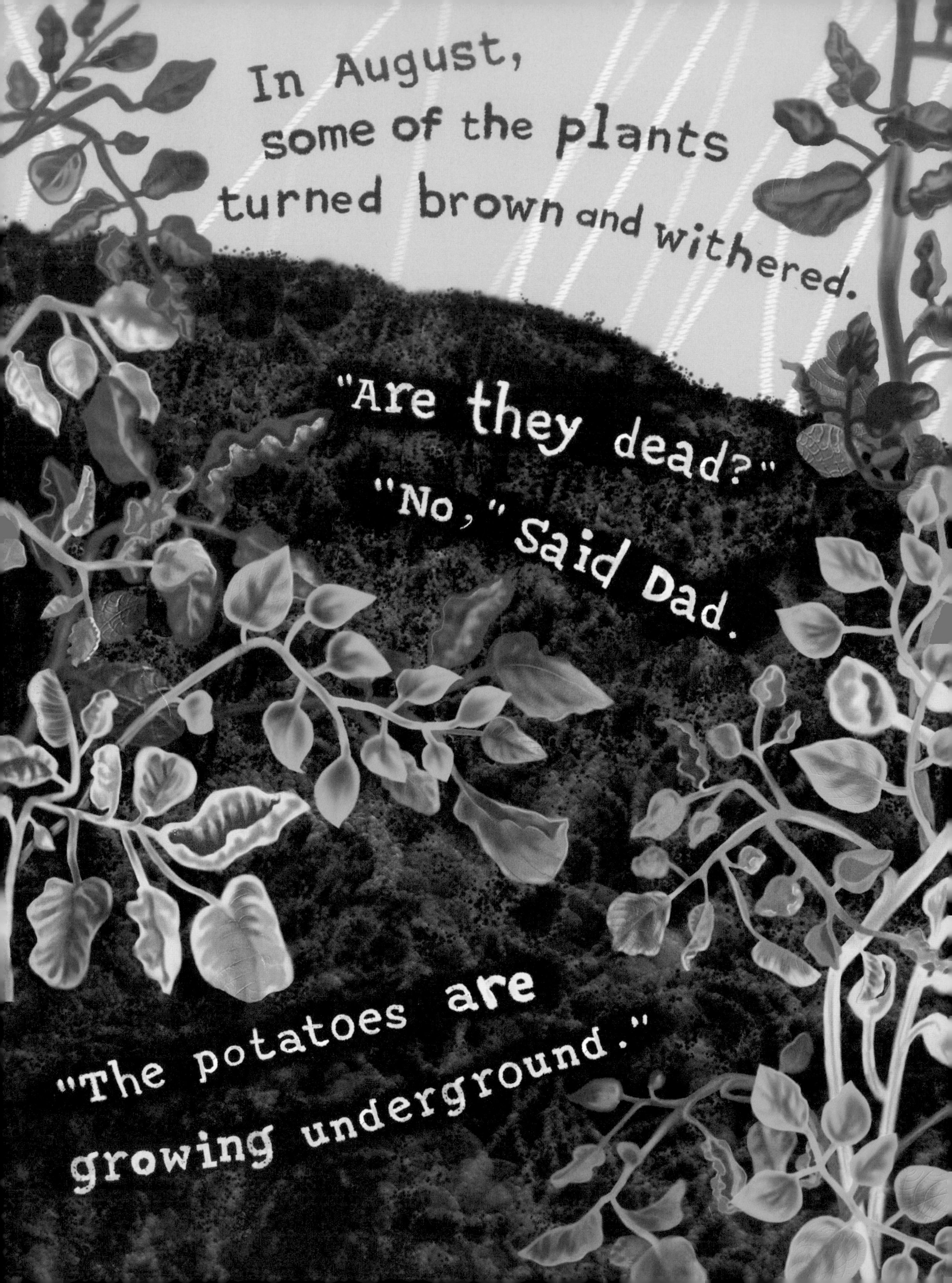

In August,
some of the plants
turned brown and withered.

"Are they dead?"
"No," Said Dad.

"The potatoes are
growing underground."

"Are you sure?"

"I hope so. That's what your grandpa said."

We weeded.

We watered.

We waited.

Now, on a cool September day,
Dad and I sit on the bench in front of the garden.
"How's your bedroom at your mom's house coming?" Dad asks.
"Good. Mom and I painted it
periwinkle."

"Periwinkle.
I like that color.
I bet it looks good."

"You can see it on Friday when you pick me up."
"Okay," Dad says. "It will be Periwinkle Friday."

We get up

and walk to the garden.

"What's your favorite way

to eat potatoes?" Dad asks.

"MASHED,

with lots of butter and

a sprinkle of nutmeg for good luck."

"Mmmmmm,
that's my
favorite,
too.
Let's see
what's under
these hills."

Dad gets the garden fork
from the shed
and I carry the big bucket.

Dad digs at the first hill.
Nothing but dirt.
He digs again. More dirt.

"After all that work,"
I say.

Dad hands me the fork.
"You try."

I dig deep. I lift the fork and see seven golden shapes.
"Potatoes!" I shout.

"LOOK at those SPUDS," Dad says.

I bend down,
pick up a potato,
rub the dirt off its skin,
and set it in the bucket.

ONE potato,

two potato,

THREE potato,

four,

Five potato,

SIX potato,

SEVEN POTATO,

more

EACH HILL HAS LOTS OF POTATOES.

SOME ARE SMALL. SOME ARE BIG.

SOME HAVE FUNNY FACES.

51 Potato, 52 Potato, 53 Potato, 54,
55 Potato, 56 Potato, 57 Potato,
More.

I count Sixty-SEVEN
and our bucket is
overflowing.

"All this from two old potatoes."
"Yes." Dad rubs my head.
"Ready to dig in to the potatoes you grew?"
"Yeah, I'm hungry."

# Mashed Potatoes

2 pounds of potatoes (Yukon Golds are a favorite)
1/2 teaspoon of salt
1/2 stick (4 tablespoons) of butter
1/2 cup of milk (heated)
A sprinkle of nutmeg

Peel the potatoes and cut them into equal-sized cubes.
Put the potatoes in a pan, cover with cold water, and add the salt.
Bring the water to a boil, reduce the heat, and simmer until the potatoes are tender.
Drain the potatoes in a colander.
Return the potatoes to pan and heat for one minute to dry.
Turn off the heat and stir the potatoes with a wooden spoon.
Mash with a masher.
Add the butter.
Mash some more.
Add the hot milk.
Stir until smooth with the wooden spoon.
Add a sprinkle of nutmeg for good luck.

Enjoy!